CROSS-COUNTRY
CONSPIRACY

BY JAKE MADDOX

text by
Daniel Mauleón

STONE ARCH BOOKS
a capstone imprint

Published by Stone Arch Books, an imprint of Capstone.
1710 Roe Crest Drive
North Mankato, Minnesota 56003
capstonepub.com

Library of Congress Cataloging-in-Publication Data
Names: Maddox, Jake, author. | Mauleón, Daniel, 1991– author.
Title: Cross-country conspiracy / Jake Maddox ; text by Daniel Mauleón.
Description: North Mankato, MN : Stone Arch Books, an imprint of Capstone, 2022. |
Series: Jake Maddox JV mysteries | Audience: Ages 8–11. | Audience: Grades 4–6. |
Summary: Twins Domingo and Carmen Rivera are ready for the big Mega Meet, when
the four camps compete in an annual cross-country running competition. But this year
there are problems: in the boys' race there is a pile-up, and Andy, Domingo's old friend,
manages to prevent him from winning. When Andy sends a text warning Carmen to
watch out in the girls' race, the twins become convinced that some of the other kids
are cheating by working together to sabotage rival runners.
Identifiers: LCCN 2021012618 (print) | LCCN 2021012619 (ebook) | ISBN 9781663920270
(paperback) | ISBN 9781663911117 (hardcover) | ISBN 9781663911087 (ebook pdf)
Subjects: LCSH: Twins—Juvenile fiction. | Brothers and sisters—Juvenile fiction. |
Cross-country running—Juvenile fiction. | Sports—Corrupt practices—Juvenile fiction. |
Detective and mystery stories. | CYAC: Mystery and detective stories. | Running—Fiction.
| Twins—Fiction. | Brothers and sisters—Fiction. | Racing—Fiction. | Cheating—Fiction.
| LCGFT: Sports fiction. | Detective and mystery fiction.
Classification: LCC PZ7.M25643 Cs 2021 (print) | LCC PZ7.M25643 (ebook) | DDC 813.6
[Fic]—dc23
LC record available at https://lccn.loc.gov/2021012618
LC ebook record available at https://lccn.loc.gov/2021012619

Editorial Credits
Editor: Amber Ross; Designer: Tracy Davies; Media Researcher: Jo Miller; Production
Specialist: Katy LaVigne

Image Credits: Shutterstock/WoodysPhotos, cover

Printed and bound in the USA. 4270

TABLE OF CONTENTS

CHAPTER 1

CAMP EAGLE

The bus bumped down the dusty trail to Camp Eagle. Carmen looked out the bus window. She watched as they turned a corner and a shimmering lake came into view. She couldn't see it completely. Part of the lake was blocked by trees and a half-dozen cabins. Still, the early morning sunlight bounced off the surface of the water. Soon the rest of the camp was visible too: a big green field with a thick forest beyond that.

Carmen looked across the aisle at her brother, Domingo. His body bobbed with the motion of the bus. His eyes were closed, and she could hear the faint sound of music coming from his earbuds.

"Domingo, wake up, we're here," Carmen told her brother.

"I am awake," he said sleepily.

"Well then get moving! I want to take a look around."

Domingo stretched and yawned. Then, barely opening his eyes, he stood up and grabbed his duffel bag. Carmen grabbed her own bag and set off up the aisle. Her drowsy brother followed along behind her.

Carmen hopped off the bus and into the bright summer day and took a deep breath. Then she heard a *thump thump* and quickly stepped out of the way as Domingo nearly fell out of the bus. The sunlight reflected off the lake and onto his face. He squinted, holding his arm up to cover his eyes.

Carmen pushed her brother toward the rest of the campers who just got off the bus. "Let's get a move on, little bro."

"Five minutes!" Domingo snapped. "You are only five minutes older!"

Carmen smiled. She knew their twin rivalry would be enough to finally start shaking him awake.

Walking side by side, it was pretty obvious they were twins. They both had dark curly hair, although Carmen's was much longer and ended just above her shoulders. And after spending nearly the entire summer outside, their normally light-brown skin had tanned to a warm copper.

Usually they would stand apart in their personal fashion sense. Carmen typically wore her trademark hoodie, and Domingo sported a different band tee for each day of the month. But since they were both here to race, they wore matching Camp Loon cross-country uniforms: a black sleeveless track shirt with a printed loon and short shorts.

Carmen shivered as a breeze from the field blew past. She had left her hoodie at Camp Loon, and she already regretted it.

"So, this is Camp Eagle," Carmen said as the two walked from the bus lot to an open-air dining area.

"It doesn't look much different from Camp Loon," replied Domingo. He put his headphones away in his duffel.

The twins had spent the last month of the summer at Camp Loon. During the day they trained for cross-country, and at night they played games, told ghost stories, and hung out with the other campers. But the whole month had led up to today.

Camp Loon was part of a larger program of camps including Hawk, Blue Jay, and Eagle. And on the last Saturday of the summer session, all four camps gathered for the Mega Meet. To Carmen, and probably most of the campers, the Mega Meet was what she had spent all camp thinking about. It was a way to see how much you had improved over the past month.

And of course there were the prizes. The fastest runners during each of the boys' and girls' races would win four tickets to the water park. After a summer of running outdoors, nothing sounded better. But there was another big reason Carmen and Domingo wanted to win today.

The siblings had a tradition of recording each other's races. Afterward, they would watch the footage and talk about how to improve. However, their cell phone cameras were not the best at this. Their parents had made a deal with the twins before camp started: they would buy the kids a better camera if they won their races. It encouraged Carmen and her brother to take camp seriously and train hard.

Carmen was deep in a camera-shopping daydream when she reached the information tables. One of their camp counselors, Larry, outlined the schedule for the day. Larry was a very tall high schooler who wore sunglasses all day—even inside.

Larry acted like he was the "cool" counselor, but if you asked the other campers, that title was up for debate.

"Y'all ready to run?" Larry asked.

The crowd of campers mostly groaned. Carmen glanced at them. Like her brother, they all looked pretty tired from staying up late telling ghost stories. Carmen had made a point to go to bed early, in preparation for today.

Larry ignored the campers and continued. "The boys' race will be starting at nine a.m. That's a half hour from now. The girls' race will start at ten-thirty. Afterward there will be a big all-camp barbecue before we hop back on the bus to Camp Loon."

As Larry talked, Carmen heard the rumble of other buses. She turned to see the buses from Camp Hawk and Camp Blue Jay roll in. Meanwhile the Eagle campers were filing out of their cabins to check out their competition.

"Ugh, they act like they own the place," Carmen muttered to her brother.

"Why do you say that?" Domingo asked.

Carmen gestured with her head in the direction of an Eagle camper. The girl had her arms crossed and was glaring at Carmen, and now her brother. When Domingo made eye contact, the Eagle camper smirked. Domingo gave a big goofy wave.

"Why would you do that?" Carmen hissed.

Domingo shrugged. "I dunno. To cut the tension," he said, turning away from the Eagle campers. "Now let's go take a look at the course."

"Whatever," Carmen replied, "Let's look around."

"That's what I just said!" Domingo replied.

They left their duffel bags on the table and headed toward the start of the racecourse.

"I don't know why you let other people bother you like that," Domingo said as they walked past the cabins.

"It just seems silly to have an attitude. I mean this Mega Meet is cool and all, but it's not like it's the world championship or something," Carmen answered.

"Whatever," Domingo said, giving an exaggerated shrug. "I just let that stuff brush right off me."

Carmen rolled her eyes. He was right, however. It did her no good to get upset ahead of a race. But she also knew her brother. They were twins, after all. Underneath his carefree, playful attitude, he took running as seriously as she did. And while the other campers didn't seem to intimidate him, they were still his competition. Carmen watched from behind as her brother stepped onto the course and relaxed his body. He was focused.

"All right," he asked, "what do you see?"

The course was marked with orange cones. Together they began to walk and analyze the course. In some places the course even had boundary lines painted by the camp.

"Take a look at the path here," Carmen said. She gestured to where it moved closer to the lake. "There's much less grass, just dry, cracked dirt." She looked up and down the course. It looked to be the standard width, about six yards wide. Enough room to give runners the chance to pass each other safely.

The two kept walking. After a hundred yards or so, the course curved sharply left and followed the bend of the lake. Domingo and Carmen stood for a moment at the bend.

"This is a really sharp turn," Carmen said.

"And so early in the race," added Domingo. "Everyone is going to clump up here for the shortest route."

"They have to if they want to win," Carmen said. She thought back to one of their first lessons at Camp Loon. Even though you have lots of room on a course, there is always an ideal lane you should try to be in.

"Remember to hug the corner," they both said at the same time. They laughed and continued down the path.

For the next few hundred yards, the course followed the lake. It curved, slowly, toward the forest. Carmen and her brother entered the forest and were covered in shade. The course was just as wide in the forest. However, the dense wall of trees made everything feel cramped.

Inside the forest, the course curved slowly to the right. Once you were far enough in, you couldn't see very far ahead or behind. The ground here was a mix of grass, moss, and—*mud!* Carmen looked over to see her brother, eyes on the canopy above, inches from a puddle.

"Careful!" Carmen shouted, pulling her brother away from the muddy puddle. "Looks like the rain from last night still hasn't dried up in here." Carmen pointed ahead to a few puddles dotting the path.

"Thanks. Wouldn't want to get my kicks dirty," Domingo jokingly pointed to his shoes, which were already covered in grass stains and dirt from a summer in nature.

"Sure, you would be fine now, but at least be careful during the race," she said. "Might get a little slippery."

"Of course," he said more seriously. "As long as we keep our eyes on the ground in here it shouldn't cause too much trouble."

They continued for a few hundred yards more, keeping an eye on the muddy forest floor. After a few minutes of walking, they exited the forest. From here they could see the rest of the course. A simple run across a grassy field heading back to camp.

Suddenly the sound of a whistle cut through the air. "That's the ten-minute warning," Domingo stated. "I'd better warm up properly." Then he jogged away.

While her brother went to get ready, Carmen had other work to do. She looked around the course to decide the best spot to watch, one where she could also record the race. The field was too simple. The forest would have bad lighting.

"The bend," she said to herself. She headed back toward the lake, her cell phone in hand.

CHAPTER 2

AND THEY'RE OFF

Domingo touched his fingertips to his toes. He could feel the pull in his leg muscles. He took his time standing back up. This was the last stretch of his routine, and he used it to focus. Finally, his back straightened, he looked forward. There, ten feet away from him, was an old friend.

"Andy?" Domingo called out.

Andy turned. He was a bit shorter than Domingo but just as lanky. Andy's black hair was buzzed short.

His pale skin contrasted with the blue uniform of Camp Blue Jay.

"Domingo!" Andy responded. His eyes were open wide in excitement.

The two approached each other as if to hug it out like old friends. But as Domingo got closer, he hesitated. Andy paused a few feet away as well.

The two hadn't seen each other since sixth grade, when Andy's family had moved away. Before then, the two were practically best friends. They'd hung out in school and spent weekends racing each other at the park.

Since Andy had moved, they'd had a few video calls. Then they missed each other's birthday parties. Now, they only communicated by liking one another's photos on Instachat.

The realization hit Domingo all at once. *Do we even really know each other anymore?*

"Ha ha, this is a little weird, isn't it?" Domingo asked, cutting the tension between them.

"Yeah, a little bit," Andy said, kicking his foot into the dirt. Domingo recognized the action: one of Andy's nervous quirks.

"Let's catch up after the race," Domingo said as he held his hand up, ready for a high-five.

Andy looked away, then back again. "Yeah, after the race," he muttered. "We should line up."

Then he walked away, leaving Domingo's hand hanging.

* * *

Domingo took his place at the starting line along with the twenty-two other runners. From there, he could see the sharp left turn ahead. Unfortunately, he was starting in the far right lane. He would have to push himself a bit more than he would like to get ahead of the pack and hug the corner.

Carmen stood on the outside of the bend, waving, her cell phone camera focused on him.

Good, he thought. This first stretch would provide good footage for review. He took his starting position. He leaned down, placing his right leg behind him and bending the knee of his left.

There was a quiet in the air for a moment. Then the whistle blew. Domingo extended his left leg, pushing his foot deep against the ground and propelling him forward. Cross-country running wasn't like a usual schoolyard race. Because it took place over several miles, running too fast too early would tire you out. Instead, to be successful at cross-country, Domingo had learned to balance speed and stamina. The ideal speed was faster than a jog but slower than a sprint. Then, when a runner needed to pass another, they would push themselves just enough.

Usually, that push would be toward the end of the race. This early in the race, the runners would be all bunched up. There wasn't much room to make any big moves. However, only about a minute into the race, Domingo would need to push to take the inside lane. He wasn't the only runner who was gunning for the tight turn. After all, every runner here had been training for the past month straight. He could feel the crowd of runners shifting left. But one boy, wearing the white uniform of Camp Eagle, kept running straight, almost away from the bend.

That's weird, Domingo thought.

Domingo needed to start his push to break ahead. Otherwise he would fall behind in the crowd. It may cost him later on, but he needed to take that chance.

He counted down in his head. *Three. Two. One.*

Step by step, he increased his speed. He constantly checked over his shoulder. Domingo did not want to run into anyone.

He was almost at the front of the pack now. Only a Camp Hawk boy was still ahead of him . . . that is, until the boy started running even faster. The boy started to wobble and sway. Then he fell. Domingo quickly sidestepped to avoid the boy.

That was close, he thought.

Gasps and shouts rose up behind him. Domingo allowed himself a quick look over his shoulder. Bodies thumped and bumped into one another. The fallen boy had created a pileup.

This was not necessarily the way Domingo wanted to win, but he was now in the lead. He refocused and followed the course alongside the lake. If he could maintain his pace, the prize was certainly his.

A few minutes later, as he began to feel the burn in his muscles, Domingo entered the forest. As lovely as the sun-filled lakeside had been, it was nice to have the shade of the trees. His skin cooled and once again the air grew quiet.

Domingo could hear the crunch of another runner behind him. He quickly looked over his shoulder and saw Andy only a few yards behind. And more runners behind him.

Domingo felt a soft patch of mud and refocused. He couldn't forget: in the forest, he needed to keep his eyes on the ground. He weaved between puddles and was halfway through the woods when he heard the thumps of Andy's footsteps approaching—fast!

Soon, Andy was running alongside Domingo. If Domingo wanted to maintain his lead, he would have to speed up.

But there's more than half a mile left, Domingo thought. *I don't think I'll be able to keep up this pace for that long.*

Domingo decided to save his energy. He let Andy pass without challenge. *I'll just overtake him at the last stretch.*

After passing, Andy shifted ahead of Domingo. Then, without warning, Andy slowed down. Domingo almost crashed into him but instead stumbled to his right.

Whew, too close, Domingo thought.

No sooner had Domingo recovered from the near collision when Andy sped up and did the same thing again.

"Dude," Domingo said, confused at what was going on. He shifted farther right to avoid Andy again. Unfortunately, Domingo's focus was on Andy and not on a patch of mud ahead.

Domingo's shoes made contact with the puddle. His right foot got stuck in the thick mud, while his left slipped forward. Domingo tried to steady himself. But his legs gave way and he slammed into the ground. There was a wet thud next to him as Andy fell too. Domingo heard footsteps and laughter as a few kids passed them.

Domingo took a breath to collect himself. He was covered in mud, cold and slimy. But there was still a race to be won. He pulled himself up and stepped out of the puddle. Domingo turned to look at Andy, but Andy looked away. Then Domingo began running again. The kids who had passed him were already at the forest exit.

Domingo tried to push himself to catch up. But his body was sore from the impact and tired from the sprint at the beginning of the race. He passed a couple runners as he ran out of the forest and across the field, breathing hard. Yet try as he might, he couldn't gain on the lead runner. Exhausted and covered in mud, Domingo took second place.

CHAPTER 3

THE WINNER IS . . .

Carmen covered her mouth in surprise as she watched her brother pass the finish line, missing first place by several seconds. Based on his muddy makeover, she could guess he'd taken a tumble in the forest. As she moved near him, he bent over and placed his hands on his knees. He took deep breaths. Now only a few feet away, she could see the mud drying on his face, in his hair, and soaked into his running uniform.

"You were supposed to avoid the mud puddles," Carmen joked.

Domingo didn't laugh or fire back a response. Instead, he just stared at the ground.

"Hey," Carmen said, switching to a concerned tone, "what happened to you?"

"He happened," Domingo said, gesturing to another runner who was just crossing the finish line. Carmen looked at the boy, also caked in mud. After a moment she recognized Domingo's old friend.

"Is that Andy?"

"Yeah," Domingo spit, "He boxed me out in the forest. We both slipped into a puddle." Domingo let out a scream of frustration. "Ugh! I could have won!"

"Hey, be happy you didn't get hurt," Carmen said. And all things considered, he ended up better than most this morning. "A slip in the mud could have been much worse. You were lucky to not be in the pileup at the bend. Two kids had to go to the camp nurse."

Domingo huffed in response.

"I got footage of it if you want to review it," Carmen said, hoping to distract him. It wasn't like her brother to get this upset.

"Maybe later," Domingo said. He wasn't taking her bait. She followed his eyeline to Andy, who was wiping mud off his face with a towel.

"Be right back," Domingo said. He stomped toward Andy.

"Domingo!" Carmen said, following after her brother.

Domingo met Andy at the finish line and glared at him for a moment.

"Why did you do that?!" Domingo growled.

"I'm sorry," Andy mumbled, "I—I didn't see the mud."

"Oh, come on, man! You and I both know you were trying to get me to fall." Domingo was inches from Andy's face now.

Carmen stepped in and pulled her brother back, but he kept going.

"You could have avoided me, and we would both be okay."

"I'm sorry you didn't win," Andy said sheepishly.

"Win? I could've gotten hurt!" Domingo said.

Carmen recognized her words; she had just told Domingo the same thing.

"Is everything okay?" a voice asked from behind them.

Carmen turned around, expecting to see a camp counselor. Instead, it was a Camp Eagle boy with medium-length blond hair. He was probably half a foot taller than any of them. Unlike most of the campers here, he was packing serious muscle. Carmen recognized him as the winner of the race.

"They are just having a disagreement," Carmen said, trying to get one less person involved. But the boy just ignored her.

"I saw you two slip in the woods," he said, wincing for effect. "That didn't look good. Hope you're okay."

"We're fine, thanks," Domingo said. He didn't even turn to look at who was talking to him. Instead, he stared down Andy.

Andy tucked his hands behind his back and hung his head. He shot a quick look of concern at Carmen, then returned his gaze back down, not once looking at Domingo or the Eagle camper.

"Domingo, what are you doing?" Carmen asked, once again trying to pull her brother back.

He took a step back, and she could see his face clearly now. His anger went away, and now he was staring at the ground.

"I—I'm sorry," Domingo said. Then, shrugging off Carmen's arm, he walked away.

Carmen looked at Andy, then at the Eagle camper. Neither of them spoke.

"Uh, nice to see you, Andy," Carmen said before turning around to follow her brother.

"Okay, what was that?" Carmen said once she had caught up to her brother.

"Nothing," Domingo said. He was still walking.

"It was *not* nothing," Carmen said. "I get that you are upset that you lost, but since when do you go yelling at your friends? Macho does not suit you well."

Domingo turned around, his face twisted in emotion. Being a twin brought its own set of troubles. People were always comparing you. You had to share birthday parties. But there was also an upside—you understood your twin better than anyone else in the world.

As Carmen looked at her brother, she was grateful for this last part. Yes, she saw anger in Domingo's expression, but there was also deep embarrassment. Usually, her brother would have bounced back to his relaxed self by now. But Carmen could tell that something more than the race was digging at him.

"What?" Domingo lashed out. Carmen blinked— she must have been staring.

"First, don't talk to me like that," Carmen said, not backing down. "Second, let's get that mud off you."

Carmen led her brother to Counselor Larry, who was polishing his sunglasses.

"Hey, Larry. Can he jump in the lake?" she asked. If anyone would allow Domingo to jump in the lake, it would be Larry. Larry put on the sunglasses and looked Domingo up and down, the mud now dry.

"Just to clean off all this mud," added Domingo.

"I'll keep an eye on him," said Carmen. "I have some time before my race anyway. I'll make sure he stays in the shallow end."

Larry thought about the proposal, then he gave a slow nod of approval. Domingo grabbed his duffel from the pile Larry was watching and headed toward the dock.

A few minutes later, Carmen watched from the dock as her brother floated on top of the water. Domingo was still in his running uniform, but most of the mud had come off. He wasn't his joking self, but he had appeared to cool off. Carmen thought back to what her brother had said to Andy.

"You really think Andy did it on purpose?" Carmen asked. "What would he gain if you both fell in the mud?"

"I dunno," Domingo said, "just a feeling." Suddenly, a beep sounded from Domingo's duffel bag. Carmen looked over at the open bag.

"It's your phone," Carmen said. She pulled his phone from the bag, checking the screen. "You got a text."

"Hey, get your hands off my phone!" Domingo said, sitting up in the shallow water.

Carmen ignored him. "It's from Andy," she said, her eyes wide as she read the message. "It says, 'Tell your sister to be careful during her race. I don't want her to get hurt.'"

CHAPTER 4

OLD HABITS

Domingo lay on the dock, the sun drying him off. Carmen sat next to him, her feet dangling over the edge. He stared at his phone and his conversation with Andy.

Domingo had texted to ask: *What do you mean about Carmen?* He'd sent the text a few minutes ago and there was still no response.

"Is that a threat?" Carmen asked, "because it sounds like a threat."

Domingo didn't know how to respond. Even though he was out of the water, he felt like he was sinking, a weight growing in his stomach. He kept playing a memory in his head, one of Andy from a few summers ago.

Domingo used to go to a park near his house and run from one side to the other, timing himself. One day, when he arrived, he had found two kids doing something similar. Andy and another boy, whose name he never learned, were huffing and puffing after just sprinting across.

"You two racing?" Domingo had asked.

"Yeah . . . you got . . . a problem . . . with that?" Andy said between breaths. He had just lost the sprint, but clearly not without putting in effort.

"No problem," Domingo responded, "other than the fact that you two are pretty slow."

"Hey!" the other boy shouted.

"No way you are faster than me," Andy said, puffing up his chest.

"You want to put your money where your mouth is?" Domingo said. He fished through his pockets and held up two five-dollar bills. "Ten dollars says I can beat you, there and back."

"Nice try," Andy laughed, "we just ran a whole race. You're fresh."

"Whatever," Domingo said, putting the cash back in his pocket.

"Wait—gimmie a head start and I'll consider it," Andy responded quickly. He pulled out a wallet, and from that a ten-dollar bill. "A twenty-second head start."

"Fifteen," Domingo responded.

"Fine," Andy said. He turned to the other boy. "You want in?"

The boy looked between the two of them. "Do I get a head start too?"

"Sure," Domingo said, "you'll need it."

The boys stashed their cash, all thirty dollars, under a rock by the fence. Then they each lined up.

Domingo counted them down. "Three, two, one!"

Andy and the boy took off. Though they'd just raced, both whizzed ahead of Domingo as he counted down.

Fifteen . . . Fourteen . . . Thirteen . . .

Already the other boy was pulling ahead of Andy.

Nine . . . Eight . . . Seven . . .

Domingo's foot bounced. He was eager to run.

Three . . . Two . . . One . . .

Domingo pushed off the fence and bolted forward. As far behind as he was, he enjoyed a challenge, but the other boy was *fast* and didn't show any fatigue from the first race. So even though Domingo was gaining ground, he was in trouble.

Domingo watched as the boy touched the opposite fence and turned around. But the boy didn't see Andy right behind him. The two collided, then stumbled into the fence. It wasn't pretty. But Domingo pressed forward, reaching the fence and passing his opponents as they struggled to get back up.

"Hey—stop!" the boy shouted.

"Not my fault you wasted your head start," Domingo said, crossing back across the field. He'd reached the money in no time and turned around to see the boy and Andy screaming at him. Then he'd pocketed the cash, hopped the fence, and kept running.

"Hey, Domingo!" Carmen's voice cut through his daydream. "Domingo!" she said again. "Hello? You in there?"

Domingo's mind was brought back to the dock and his sister.

"You going to help me figure out why Andy is threatening me?" she said. "Or are you just going to daydream?"

"Are you sure it's a threat?" Domingo asked, even though he still had a pit in his stomach.

"It is absolutely a threat," Carmen responded. "And we have less than an hour to figure out what it means!"

The siblings sat in silence for a few moments. Finally, Domingo spoke.

"Maybe he's just telling you to be careful of the puddles in the forest," he offered. "It would be tough to try and push another person into those puddles. You'll be on the lookout."

"Yeah, I guess. And it's not like I'll be racing against Andy," Carmen said. "Do you really think he did it on purpose?"

The pit in Domingo's stomach grew. He had to tell her the whole story, even if he was embarrassed. It might keep her safe.

"A few summers ago, I used to run at Meadow Park," Domingo started.

"What does this have to do with anything?" Carmen said, irritated.

"Please, just listen, okay?" Domingo sat up and looked out across the lake. Carmen must have noticed the shift in his tone, because she went quiet. Domingo continued.

"Sometimes I would challenge other kids to races. Well, Andy and I would. But we would act like we didn't know each other."

"Okay, I'm listening," Carmen said, "but I don't understand."

Domingo took a deep breath and let it out slowly. There was no point talking around it.

"Andy and I used to con other kids at the park. He would race them and let them win. Then I would show up and bet money that I could beat them. Andy would convince the other kid to take the bet, and we would race. But the thing was, the first race was always supposed to tire them out and make it easy for me to win. Then afterward, Andy would meet up with me and we would split the winnings."

"Okay," Carmen said.

Domingo didn't dare look at her. He was too embarrassed.

"That's cheap, and we're going to talk about that later," she said. "But I don't exactly get what that has to do with today. You think Andy cheated? He also lost the race."

"I think he's helping someone else win," Domingo answered.

Carmen just blinked at her brother, unbelieving.

He continued, "Sometimes, when we were running our con, if there was a chance I would lose, Andy would take on the competition by tripping or knocking into them. Anything to win the bet. I think that's what he did today."

They sat on the dock in silence.

Carmen kicked at the water. "It still doesn't add up. The kid who won is from a different camp."

"And why warn you about the girls' race?" Domingo added.

"Unless some of the girls are planning on cheating too," Carmen said.

"And there's one other thing." Domingo sighed. "This scam only works with a few runners. Andy can't bump into everyone, so why bother risking it?"

"Maybe he had more help . . ." Carmen said, trailing off and picking up her phone. She tapped a few things on the screen, then held it up to her brother. She had brought up a recording.

"The pileup at the start of the race took out most of the competition. And I caught it all on camera."

CHAPTER 5

PLAY-BY-PLAY

Carmen sat next to Domingo on the edge of the

dock. She tried not to think about the scam he and

Andy had run to get other kids' money. Right now

her biggest concern was her own race.

On top of trying to win, now I have to be careful not

to get injured?

Carmen shook her head to clear her worries.

Now was not the time to get lost in anxious

thoughts.

Holding her phone so Domingo could see it too, Carmen played the start of the race. Then she fast-forwarded until the pack of runners was at the bend. She had been lucky to set herself up right at that location on the course.

Carmen paused the video. "That's him in the brown Camp Hawk uniform," she said, pointing to a boy with messy blond hair. "I heard the counselors call him Edison when they walked him back to the nurse's station." She played the video again.

They watched as the race unfolded on the small screen. First, Edison broke away from the pack.

"Look, he starts sprinting to get ahead of everyone," Domingo said. "I remember thinking that he would tire himself out by starting so hard."

Edison looked over each shoulder. Then he slowed down a bit. He looked over both shoulders again before tripping, falling sideways, and rolling to the ground. Almost immediately, the other runners began bumping into one another to avoid him. A few tripped or stepped directly on Edison, and about half of the group fell over.

"Ouch," Domingo said as Carmen paused the video.

"Maybe if he hadn't been looking over his shoulder so much, he would have avoided whatever it was that tripped him up," Carmen said.

"Yeah, maybe," Domingo said. "Can you play it again?"

Carmen went back a minute so they could watch the event unfold for a second time.

"WAIT!" Domingo shouted. "Go back a few seconds."

"I'm right next to you. No need to shout," Carmen said. They watched Edison fall for a third time.

"Pause!" Domingo yelled.

"Okay! Why don't you just take over?" Carmen handed him her phone.

"Sorry," Domingo responded, taking it from her. "I just got excited."

He adjusted the slider until it landed on the frame he was looking for.

"Look, it's the kid who won! The one from Camp Eagle," he said. "He started moving away from the turn before Edison fell."

Carmen looked closely. Sure enough, while every runner bunched up behind Edison, the Eagle camper steered away.

"You're right," she said. She reached over to tap the screen, advancing a few frames. "It's not just him. There's Andy at the back of the group, moving away from everyone."

"So it was both of them," Domingo said.

Carmen nodded. "It's like they were expecting it to happen."

"Yeah," Domingo said. "It definitely looks that way. But like you said, they're all from different camps. There's no way they planned it this morning."

"Maybe they all know each other some other way?" Carmen suggested. She looked at her phone again. She didn't have long before she needed to start getting ready.

"I still feel like we're missing a lot of information," Domingo said. "But I know who we need to talk to."

CHAPTER 6

FALL GUY

Domingo and Carmen found Edison sitting on a bench outside the nurse's station, packing his duffel bag. Edison had changed out of his running gear, and bandages covered his arms and legs. Where there weren't bandages, there were bruises. In the few spots where there weren't bruises, there was bad sunburn.

Domingo had never had a sunburn, but from the name he expected it was pretty nasty. He gathered Edison wasn't having the best summer.

When Domingo was a few feet away, Edison zipped up his bag and put his water bottle on top. The water bottle was red and had a white logo with the letters *MMS* on it. Something about it looked familiar to Domingo, but he wasn't sure why.

"That was a nasty fall," Carmen said.

Edison looked up at them for the first time.

"I saw it all happen from the sidelines," she continued.

Edison gave her a funny look. "Do I know you?"

Domingo couldn't stand the awkward tension between them.

"Sorry," he jumped in to help save the situation. "I'm Domingo, and this is my sister, Carmen. We just came over to see if you're okay."

"Hey," Edison said. "I guess I'm fine. Nothing is broken."

There was another long pause.

"Did you do it on purpose?" Carmen asked suddenly.

"Carmen!" Domingo hissed. This was not the best way to go about it.

"Do what on purpose?" Edison's face went red. "Fall and get run over?"

"Sorry, it's just, I have a video," Carmen said, pulling out her phone. "And it looks like—"

"What are you trying to say?" Edison asked.

"Err—" Domingo interrupted. "What we are trying to say is, it looks like your fall wasn't an accident."

We should have planned this better, Domingo thought.

He continued. "It looks like you tripped on purpose." He forced a caring smile. Maybe it was best to be direct.

"I can't believe you two are accusing me of—" Edison stopped talking as Carmen stuck her phone in his face.

"Really, Carmen?" Domingo said, embarrassed.

Carmen just shrugged.

Edison watched in silence as the video played. He scrunched his face in pain when he saw himself get run over.

"Why would you show me that?" Edison's voice was shaky. "I made a mistake, okay?"

Domingo and Carmen shared a quick glance.

"What do you mean, 'mistake'?" Domingo asked.

"Why did you do it?" Carmen asked at the same time.

Edison looked between the twins. He pulled his duffel bag close.

"Were you trying to help that kid from Camp Eagle?" Carmen asked.

"Did Andy give you the idea?" Domingo followed. This felt pointless—they weren't giving Edison time to respond. It was clear Domingo and Carmen had never run an interrogation before.

"You two should be ashamed," a girl's voice came from behind the twins.

Domingo and his sister turned around to see a Camp Hawk runner. Her dark brown eyes stared them both down. The fact that she was just a bit taller than them made her gaze even more intimidating.

"Edison, who are these two?" the girl asked. She pushed past the twins toward Edison, her long black hair trailing behind her.

"I don't know, Novalee, they just showed up," Edison responded. His voice had steadied since she'd arrived.

Novalee spun around and pointed her finger at Domingo and Carmen. "Are all Camp Loon kids as rude as you two? Edison is in pain from a race he *lost*, and you want to blame him for that?"

Domingo froze. *She's right. What were we thinking? That we're real detectives?* He hung his head in shame and rubbed the back of his neck.

"Come on, Edison, let's get out of here before they bother you anymore," Novalee said, helping Edison get up.

Edison grabbed his duffel bag, but as he stood up, the water bottle fell onto the ground. It rolled toward Domingo.

Domingo picked it up, once again staring at the MMS logo. He looked back up at Edison and offered the bottle.

Domingo forced out a feeble "sorry." Then the two Camp Hawk kids walked away without another word.

"Ugh!" Carmen said. "I felt like he was about to tell us something."

Domingo didn't respond. Something about that water bottle stuck with him. He pulled out his phone and started typing into the search bar.

Carmen continued, "If she's right, and we are just making this all up, we just yelled at an injured runner for losing. What a waste of time!"

"Maybe not." Domingo held out his phone. "My cell phone signal hasn't been great out here, but there is open Wi-Fi coming from the nurse's station. Look what I just found online."

Carmen stepped closer to better see her brother's phone. Domingo had pulled up a school's website. At the top was a red banner with the letters *MMS*. The letters and color matched the style of Edison's water bottle. Carmen read the name underneath the letters, "Maryland Middle School."

"That's Andy's school," Domingo said.

CHAPTER 7

FAST FRIENDS

Carmen sat on the bench outside the nurse's station, tapping away at her phone. Her brother sat next to her, also focused on his device.

"We need something . . ." he muttered.

". . . just a single clue linking the two of them," Carmen said, finishing her brother's thought.

She was poking around the Maryland Middle School website, seeing if their cross-country team had any photos or even names of their runners.

But it looked like most of the pages hadn't been updated in years.

Domingo, on the other hand, had chosen to scroll through Andy's Instachat feed. "Here!" he said excitedly. "I had to get through a month's worth of camp photos, but I finally found one of Andy and Edison."

"That's definitely Edison," Carmen said, looking at the photo. In it, Andy and Edison had their arms over each other's shoulders and were looking down at the camera, almost as if they were in a huddle. Edison's hair was a bit shorter then. But it was easily the same kid who had been sitting on the bench just a few minutes ago.

"Is Edison tagged in the photo?" Carmen asked.

"Nope. He must not have an account. But there is a hashtag."

There at the bottom of the photo was the hashtag #MMSXC.

"I wonder what it stands for," Domingo said.

"I'm guessing it stands for Maryland Middle School Cross-country," Carmen said, still looking at her brother's phone.

Domingo clicked the hashtag, and it brought up a series of photos that had the same tag.

"Look at this," Carmen said. She reached out and scrolled on her brother's phone. The tagged photos were various group shots of Andy, Edison, and Novalee. There were also two other girls and one boy who showed up repeatedly.

"I would be able to if you weren't in my way!" Domingo said, pulling his phone out of her grip.

"Touchy," Carmen said.

"Isn't that the Eagle camper who won?" Domingo asked. He tilted his phone so his sister could take a look.

Carmen stared at it. The boy did look similar, but much shorter.

"If it's him, he definitely had a growth spurt," she said.

Domingo tapped on the photo, revealing the usernames of everyone tagged. "His name is Maverick."

"Did you see either of those other girls this morning?" Carmen asked.

"I don't think so." Domingo clicked on their tags. "This is Hannah, and the other girl is Mikayla."

"What's Hannah's username?" Carmen asked, pulling up Instachat on her own phone.

Domingo looked at the name. "HannahXC."

"Found her!" Carmen said quickly. "See, this is why you have to keep your account private."

Domingo rolled his eyes. "Yours isn't."

"Well no, but I'm not cheating at cross-country races," Carmen said.

"You don't know they are cheating," Domingo said, having resumed scrolling on his phone.

Carmen knew he was right. They knew nothing. All they had was a hunch based on Andy's history, Domingo's race, and that threatening text.

"Hey, look at this," Carmen said. She held her phone out to her brother. "Hannah is at Camp Blue Jay with Andy."

Domingo looked at his sister's phone. Hannah was even shorter than Andy, with a face full of freckles that matched her short red hair.

"So, she must be here," Carmen continued. "I wonder if Mikayla is too?"

"Whoops," Domingo said.

"Whoops? What do you mean, 'whoops'?" Carmen asked.

"I went to click on Mikayla to see her account and accidentally liked her photo instead."

"Domingo!" Carmen exclaimed.

"I know. I know. But at least I found a photo of her in Camp Eagle gear."

"Really?" Carmen exclaimed. "Let me see!"

Domingo held up his phone.

Carmen looked at a black screen. "Uh, what photo?"

Domingo took his phone back. "Huh, it was just here. I wonder if . . . Did the Wi-Fi stop working for you?"

"No, why?"

"No photos are loading. I thought maybe I had lost the connection," Domingo said, confused.

Carmen had a sudden gnawing feeling in her stomach. "Try refreshing her account."

"I can't even find her account," Domingo said, frantically tapping his phone.

"What about Hannah?" Carmen asked. She refreshed Hannah's account on her own phone. It loaded, no problem.

"I can't find Hannah either," Domingo said.

"Novalee?" she asked.

"Nope," Domingo said. "I can't see any of their accounts anymore. Except for Andy's."

Carmen stood up in a panic. "It's not your signal, Domingo. They blocked you after you liked that photo."

Great, she thought, *now I can add online stalking to the things I'm not proud of today.*

"You're right," Domingo said, standing. "But this is good news."

"How is this good news?" Carmen asked.

"Because we know they're talking to each other. Only Mikayla was tagged in that photo I accidentally liked. She's the only one who would have gotten the notification. And they all blocked me."

Carmen started to walk away from the nurse's station. She bit at her thumbnail, deep in thought. *They are all close friends. And they are all here today. But can I really jump to conclusions about them cheating?*

"Hey, Carmen," Domingo said, catching up to her. "What are you doing?"

"Shh," she said. "I'm thinking."

They walked in silence until they got to the lakeshore. Unlike the sandy beach of the swimming area, this shoreline was covered in rocks. Carmen leaned down and picked up a smooth stone. She tossed it into the lake, and it skipped across the water. *Once. Twice. PLUNK.*

She finally spoke. "Okay, we know all six of them are close friends," Carmen started slowly.

"And all of them are here today," Domingo continued.

"Andy and Hannah from Camp Blue Jay," Carmen said, finding a rhythm.

"Novalee and Edison from Camp Hawk."

"And Maverick and Mikayla are here from Camp Eagle."

"Right," Domingo said.

Carmen hesitated before saying, "Domingo, do you really think this is some sort of conspiracy? That Andy would convince the others to cheat?"

"Honestly," Domingo said, "I'm not sure." He knelt down to look at the rocks. "We stopped after running the scam a few times. Made us both feel gross, and for what? Fifteen dollars across the summer? It wasn't worth it."

"Yeah," Carmen agreed.

Domingo picked up a rock and handed it to his sister. "But if they win the boys' *and* girls' races, they'll have eight VIP water park passes. That's worth at least a couple hundred dollars."

Carmen skipped the rock across the water. *Once. Twice. Three times. PLUNK.*

"Based on my video, it looks like Edison threw the race. And Maverick and Andy were expecting it, because they ran around the pileup," Carmen said.

"Andy definitely helped Maverick win when he tried to box me out," Domingo added.

"Based on Andy's warning," Carmen continued, "there's a chance Novalee, Hannah, and Mikayla will try something during my race. But it is still just a hunch."

She found another flat rock on the shore. She picked it up and skipped it. *Once. Twice. PLUNK.*

"Since they might try the same trick, you could always go on the outside corner like Maverick did,"

Domingo offered. "Then try to keep your distance for the rest of the course."

Carmen thought about this for a moment. "If I did that and won, I would still feel guilty. It isn't a real win if the other runners are being cheated." She grabbed a rock from the shore. "We could try reporting it."

"To Counselor Larry?" Domingo asked. "He wouldn't take us seriously, and what if we're wrong? What if we've blown this all out of proportion and we got them into trouble for nothing?"

Carmen sighed. He said exactly what she was thinking. She threw another stone, but it splashed straight into the lake. *He's right; we don't have any evidence.*

Carmen jumped as a whistle cut across the camp.

"That's the ten-minute warning," Carmen said. "I've got to get ready."

Domingo picked up a final stone and tossed it into the water, not even attempting to skip it. *PLUNK.*

"However this shakes out, when I'm done with my race, I'm teaching you to skip rocks," Carmen said.

"I wasn't trying to skip it. I was making a wish," Domingo replied.

Carmen gave her brother a puzzled look.

He continued, "I've got an idea. A foolish one. And I'll need all the luck I can get to pull it off."

"Oh," Carmen said, curious. "Well, tell me quickly before I have to get ready."

"First, I'll need your phone. I need to send some texts."

CHAPTER 8

THE GAMBIT

Domingo walked quickly around the camp. After a minute of searching, he found who he was looking for. Edison was sitting near the buses.

Domingo tapped a few things on his phone, then placed it carefully in his duffel. Then he approached.

"Hey, Edison. It's me again. Domingo," he said.

"What do you want?" Edison asked. He didn't sound nervous like last time. He sounded defiant.

"I—I wanted to apologize," Domingo started. "My sister and I were rude to you earlier. We didn't know the full story. We do now."

"Full story?" Edison asked, sounding confused. "I told you before, I didn't trip on purpose."

Domingo tried to match Edison's confidence. "Look, you can drop the act," Domingo said. He tried his best to keep his voice steady. "Andy told me what you all are up to."

Edison tilted his head. "I don't know what you're talking about."

Domingo reached into his jacket pocket and pulled out a phone. On it was a text conversation. At the top of the screen was Andy's name.

Domingo took a breath, then held out the phone for Edison to read.

Tell your sister to be careful during her race. I don't want her to get hurt

what's going on?

you running something?

I can't say

look man, we just want in

Plus the prize is four tickets for each race.
There is room for us two.

it will look better if
Carmen helps this time

I'll talk to Maverick

okay

we're good

have Carmen "help out" in the forest

cool.
let's catch up at the BBQ

Domingo scrolled through the conversation
so Edison could read it. Now was the hard part.
Domingo sat down next to Edison, setting his
duffel bag between them.

"Like I said, you can drop the act. My sister and I are part of the team."

Edison didn't say anything for a long moment. Then he let out a big sigh. "Whew—I did not like keeping up that lie."

Domingo laughed and put his arm on Edison's shoulder. "You did a good job. I know I'm going to talk to Andy during the barbeque, but I gotta know. How did y'all come up with this?"

"Honestly," Edison said leaning back, "it started as a joke. Andy told us about how he and an old friend used to scam people. And we've done a few things during the season. But it's easy to catch when you're on the same team. When we got our camp placements we kept joking that we should run the scam at the Mega Meet. Andy, Maverick, and Mikayla kept brainstorming and then the rest of us got on board."

"Novalee and . . ." Domingo said, trailing off.

"Hannah," Edison finished for him. "She's at Camp Blue Jay."

Domingo nodded. "So they convinced you to take the fall? You definitely drew the short straw."

"Heh, yeah. But it was important to save Maverick and Andy. They are the better runners," Edison said.

"It doesn't hurt too bad," he added. His actions said otherwise as he winced a bit.

"I'm sorry," Domingo said.

"Like I said, I'm okay," Edison said.

He seemed to have really warmed up to Domingo, which made the next part harder.

"Not that," Domingo said, then reached into his duffel bag. He pulled out his phone. "I'm sorry for tricking you."

Edison looked at Domingo's hands, each with a phone in it. "I don't understand."

"I recorded a video of our whole conversation, including your confession. My sister and I figured something was wrong. But we couldn't prove it."

"But Andy's texts," Edison said, clearly shocked.

"I changed my name in my sister's phone to Andy. Then I texted her to fake the conversation."

"I'm not sure how you can think you're better than us," Edison said, his face reddening. "I know you're the 'old friend' that used to cheat kids with Andy all the time."

Domingo winced. Edison was right—he had done some bad things growing up. *What right do I have to call out anyone else?*

Edison seized on Domingo's hesitation and lunged at him. Edison tried to grab the phone, but Domingo backed away swiftly.

"Chill out, man!" Domingo shouted, now a few feet away.

"You lied to me," Edison growled. But before he could go after Domingo again, he doubled over in pain.

"Look, I am not happy about it either. But look at you," Domingo gestured toward Edison. "You're hurt. We need to make sure your friends don't cheat again. You got lucky. You only have some scrapes and bruises."

Domingo pointed at the starting line. "My sister, Novalee, Hannah, and Mikayla might not be so lucky. Not to mention all the other kids you put at risk!"

A timer went off on Domingo's phone. One minute until the race. He looked at Edison. The boy had tears pooling in his eyes.

"Sorry," he said to Edison. "I have to go."

Domingo turned and sprinted toward the course. He didn't know if there was anything he could do to stop the cheating. Nevertheless, he had to warn Carmen.

CHAPTER 9

STARTING LINE

Carmen was in her starting position. She was on the favorable side of the course for the bend. Unfortunately, that would only matter if this was a fair race. With Novalee, Hannah, and Mikayla running, there was still too much up in the air.

She took a breath and looked up and down the line. Novalee was closest; two spots to the right of Carmen. Hannah and Mikayla were farther down the line.

"Carmen!"

Carmen looked up to see Domingo calling her from the sidelines.

He pointed to her phone. "I got it!" he shouted. "I've got proof! You have to stop them!"

I'm not sure how he did it, but I need to do something, Carmen thought. She turned to the girl next to her, a Blue Jay camper.

"Trade places?" Carmen asked. "I need to talk to her." She pointed at Novalee.

The girl shrugged and swapped spots. Now Carmen was next to Novalee.

"What do you want?" Novalee asked.

"Hey, Novalee," Carmen started, "I'm sorry about earlier. But my brother and I know you are all up to something. And now he has proof."

"Sure he does," Novalee said sarcastically.

Carmen tried to push through. "Look, I don't know you, but—"

"Just stop talking," Novalee said.

"Novalee!"

Both Carmen and Novalee jumped.

Edison was screaming from the sidelines, standing next to Domingo. "Don't do it, Novalee! You could get hurt!"

Carmen looked from Edison to Domingo and back to Novalee. The girl was in shock.

Then the starting whistle blew. Carmen was frozen, as was Novalee. Carmen wasn't sure what would happen next, but she had to at least try to race. She dug her shoes into the grass and started running.

Carmen saw Hannah a little bit ahead of her, sprinting. She was heading toward the bend.

She's going to trip, Carmen thought. She then looked to her right and saw Mikayla. Mikayla was already moving out of the way of the future pileup.

Carmen kept running. *What else can I do? If Hannah falls, a lot of runners could be injured. But if I catch up to Hannah, maybe I can convince her not to do it.*

"Hannah!"

The shout came loud and clear from behind Carmen. She craned her neck and saw that Novalee had stopped running altogether.

"Hannah!" Novalee shouted again. "It's not worth it!"

Carmen saw Hannah start to slow. She was no longer pushing to be at the front of the pack.

We did it, Carmen thought. *We prevented another pileup.*

But there was still a race to win. Carmen moved farther left to hug the corner. Now there would be no risk. Mikayla had moved too far away from the corner and started falling behind.

Serves her right, Carmen thought.

After hugging the bend, Carmen was in first place running alongside the lake. The chemical endorphins her body produced while running started filling her with joy. *I could win this. I just need to finish strong.*

Carmen kept a steady pace as the grass course changed to dirt and entered the forest.

With no distractions, Carmen easily avoided the muddy patches. She only had two challengers who tried to pass her. One was a fellow Loon camper who got stuck in some mud. The other, a girl from Camp Hawk, sped past her but didn't have the stamina to keep going. Eventually, Carmen passed her as well.

After a few minutes, Carmen could see the forest exit. Soon she would be in the final stretch.

Suddenly, there was movement between the trees. A few yards ahead, Mikayla hopped out of the forest and onto the course. She must have found a shortcut. Now Carmen was in second place going into the final stretch.

The sun burned Carmen's eyes as she left the dark forest and began the last leg of the race. This section was the simplest—there were some very light hills, but it was otherwise a straight shot forward to the finish line.

The only challenge was getting past Mikayla, twenty yards ahead. Her shortcut had granted

Mikayla a significant lead. But Carmen had to hold on to hope.

If Mikayla and the rest of her crew have spent the summer plotting to cheat, maybe they haven't spent much time training.

Carmen dismissed the thought. The only thing she should worry about now was her own running.

If she wanted to overtake Mikayla, she would have to be precise. If she pushed too hard, she might burn out before the race was over. She had to choose the perfect moment to strike. As she ran, she watched Mikayla's form. *She moves her arms too much*, Carmen thought, *and her strides aren't solid*.

Even without pushing herself, Carmen was slowly gaining on Mikayla. After a few minutes, only ten yards separated them. And with maybe thirty yards to go, this was Carmen's chance.

CHAPTER 10

FINISH LINE

Domingo watched from the finish line, his body tense in anticipation. Through the first part of Carmen's race, his adrenaline was pumping from stopping the con. Now he was on edge waiting to see if his sister would win. Mikayla had exited the forest first, but now that they were nearly fifteen yards from the finish line, Carmen had almost caught up.

Domingo zoomed his cell phone camera in on his sister as she extended her strides. Carmen's face tightened. *She must be pushing her muscles to their breaking point*, Domingo thought.

Soon Carmen was five yards behind Mikayla. Then two. Then they were neck and neck. Domingo held his breath. Mikayla stole a glance back and saw her competition. She started to sprint. But after a few seconds, she seized up.

She looks exhausted, Domingo thought.

He watched as Carmen breezed past her and across the finish line.

Domingo crashed the finish line to high-five his sister. "You did it!" he said. "Carmen, you won!"

Carmen tried to respond, but all she could do was take in deep breaths. She leaned forward, putting her hands on her knees. She smiled at her brother.

"I gotta say I'm impressed Mikayla actually got into second place. She must be a decent runner."

Carmen shook her head. "She didn't."

"She cut through the forest, didn't she?" It was Andy who had approached the two. "There's a shortcut Maverick and Mikayla found as a backup. It skips nearly a third of the course."

Domingo was surprised to see his old friend.

Are we even friends anymore?

"Hey, Domingo. Hey, Carmen," Andy said. "Look, I want to apologize for everything. For ruining our race. For lying to you. For the text that was kind of threatening. I talked with Edison. He told me how you both figured it out. And honestly, I'm thankful. The guilt has been killing me."

"Andy," Domingo said, not sure what else to say.

"Sure, that's great," Carmen said, having finally caught her breath. "But what are you going to do about it?"

"Carmen!" Domingo said, surprised his sister spoke so plainly.

"No, she's right," Andy said. "We cheated today and people got hurt. Look, when you yelled at me earlier, it took me right back to when we used to do this together. I got so caught up in the excitement of planning it that I forgot how terrible it felt on this side. I talked to the counselors already about today's races. I'm not sure what they'll do about it, but it was the right thing."

Domingo knew the guilt that Andy was talking about.

"Also," Andy said, smiling now, "the counselors are disqualifying Maverick's win from this morning's race. That makes you the winner, Domingo. Congrats, bud." Andy held out his hand for a high five.

Domingo returned his friend's gesture.

* * *

With camp a week behind them, Domingo and Carmen stood outside a house in their neighborhood. Domingo tapped his foot on the ground. He was more nervous than even before a run.

"Are you sure this is the right house?" Carmen asked.

"Yeah, I think so. I don't remember all the kids we tricked. But I'm sure one of them lived here."

"But do you know if he still lives here?"

Domingo nodded. He had seen the boy just a few days ago.

"Well," Carmen nudged her brother, "go on."

Domingo walked up to the door and knocked. There was no sound inside. He rang the doorbell. Nothing.

"I don't think he's home," Domingo called to his sister.

"All right, well just leave them and let's go home," she called back from the sidewalk.

Domingo fished in his pockets for the four tickets to the water park and tucked them under the door. Then he walked away. It didn't necessarily make things right, but it was a start.

ABOUT THE AUTHOR

Daniel Mauleón is not very good at running, much less for long periods of time. But he does enjoy reading and writing mysteries. Daniel graduated from Hamline University with a Master's in Fine Arts for Writing for Children and Young Adults in 2017 and has written a variety of books and graphic novels since. He lives with his wife and two cats in Minneapolis, Minnesota.

GLOSSARY

collision (kuh-LISH-uhn)—when two things run into each other

con (KAHN)—a dishonest trick to get money

conspiracy (kuhn-SPEER-uh-see)—a secret, dishonest plan made by two or more people

disqualify (dis-KWAHL-uh-fy)—to prevent someone from taking part in or winning an activity; athletes can be disqualified for breaking the rules of their sport

endorphins (en-DAWR-finz)—chemicals released by the body when working out

footage (FOOT-ij)—actions recorded on video

guilt (GILT)—a bad feeling inside of you because you know you did something wrong

interrogation (in-TUR-uh-gay-shun)—asking questions in a forceful way, especially of a suspect

leg (LEG)—a part of a race

sidelines (SAHYD-lahynz)—outside of the racetrack or path

stamina (STAM-uh-nuh)—the energy and strength to keep doing something for a long time

DISCUSSION QUESTIONS

1. Have you ever been in a situation when other kids were doing something you knew wasn't right? Did you go along with it or did you stand up to them?

2. Carmen made a comment that Hannah should have kept her social media account private. What types of information should be kept off of social media? What kinds of information, when shared on social media, can affect a person's safety?

3. Why do you think some people cheat? Have you ever cheated or been tempted to cheat?

WRITING PROMPTS

1. Write about a time you did something you weren't proud of. What, if anything, did you do to make it better?

2. Pretend you are a news reporter covering the Mega Meet. Write an article about the conspiracy.

3. Imagine Domingo left a note with the water park tickets. Write what it would say.

MORE ABOUT CROSS-COUNTRY

Cross-country running originated from a game called "hare and hounds." One runner, the hare, would have a head start, and would leave a trail of paper for the other runners, the hounds.

In the United States, the USA Track & Field organization holds national meets four times a year. There are different races for men, women, junior men, and junior women.

The distance of courses can vary, with some courses requiring different laps. Courses are usually between 2.5 and 7.5 miles long, with middle school and high school courses on the shorter side.

For longer events, there must be at least 440 yards of a course before the first turn. This makes sure there is enough room for runners. Shorter races don't need to follow this rule.

Because terrain, layout, and length vary so much from course to course, it is hard to track speed records.

Many cross-country events are team based, where each place (first, second, third) is given a different set of points. A team can win even if their best runner doesn't come in first.

SOLVE ALL THE SPORTS MYSTERIES!

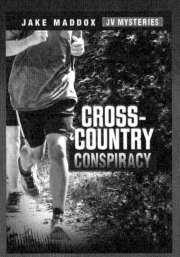

JAKE MADDOX   JV MYSTERIES

CROSS-COUNTRY
CONSPIRACY

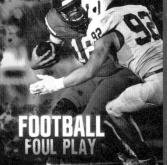

JAKE MADDOX   JV MYSTERIES

FOOTBALL
FOUL PLAY

JAKE MADDOX   JV MYSTERIES

FULL-COURT
MESS

JAKE MADDOX   JV MYSTERIES

GYMNASTICS
PAYBACK